A Tale of Ducks & Cotton

DRU MORRIS

ISBN: 978-1-008-94744-3
Imprint: Lulu.com

DEDICATION

To All Taylorians: past, present, and future.

CONTENTS

PREFACE

As I'm sure you will discover a few paragraphs into the first chapter, this book is really incredible. By incredible, I mean *without credit.* False. No citations. Completely made-up. Well . . . not completely. A few stories have a tinge of reality I couldn't quite scrape off. Kinda like that gunk left on plastic cups after you remove the clearance-price sticker. I am sorry. My goal is that you won't be able to tell the fantasy from reality. If you're ever unsure which is which, I made a list of the pesky true-facts in the Epilogue. Check it out if you're not sure what to believe.

Now, I realize some people might say, why write (or read) a book of made-up history? Why not write (or read) a book about Taylor's *real* history?

My answer? Other people have, and you should research Taylor's real history before continuing here. I'll wait . . . .

Well, now we can continue – enjoy!

CHAPTER 1 – FOUNDING OF TAYLOR

Taylor was founded in 1876, most likely before you were born. So, let's review a few facts to set the scene. The Battle of the Alamo was fought 40 years prior. The Civil War ended about 10 years ago. Texas is still mostly empty space. The University of Texas has yet to be established, but the Texas Agricultural and Mechanical College was opening its doors. You can't drive a car, but you can take a train. That happens to be where Taylor's story begins.

The Railroad

The railroad was laid down through the area a half-decade earlier, but in 1875, no station existed in Taylor's soon-to-be location. In fact, conductors despised the boring trip between Round Rock and Rockdale, and often used the 45 mile stretch of track to take a quick nap, eat a sandwich, or write in their journals.

Jimmy Johanisson, one such conductor, wrote in his diary:

> *"And now, we have entered the land between the 'Rocks'. I've ventured this line at least a dozen times, and it has never failed to provide an opportunity to dream of a more fulfilling life."*

However, the plain and simple nature of the area soon changed. It just so happened that on the 23rd of May, 1875, a flock of some twenty-thousand ducks returned to one of their seasonal roosting grounds about sixteen miles east of Round Rock. To this day zoologists cannot explain why the ducks would congregate in the grassy plain. Only a small creek cut across it, and the nearest lake was miles away. But, for whatever reason, the ducks did gather there, and had done so on-and-off for centuries.

Steam locomotive encountering ducks prior to the building of the railroad station.

When the first train plowed through the flock of ducks, an estimated two hundred of the fowl were killed. Trains were relatively new creations in the region, and these ducks had not yet learned to avoid them. The gaggle was so dense that the conductor was forced to bring the steam engine to a halt so its smokestack could be cleared of well-cooked duck carcasses.

While the passengers were inconvenienced by the five-hour delay, they did enjoy snacking on the smoked duck – samples of which were distributed to each railcar. One car on this historic train happened to be filled with a contingent of Czech tailors who, as fate would have it, specialized in duck-feathers. Delighted by their luck, they debarked the train and began their new life right there in the center of the flock.

The Tailors

Current Taylor citizen Hana Dusek, born 1925, had a grandfather on that railcar. She tells this of Ctirad Dusek's account of the historic day.

> *"There were thirty or forty of them in the rail car, playing polka music and eating kolaches on their way from Austin to a Czech settlement in the east, when suddenly they felt the train coming to a stop. At first they feared it was bandits or Indians, but looking out the windows, all they saw were ducks! Thousands and thousands of them! Since ducks were what they had worked with back in Europe, they put it to a*

vote and decided to settle right then and there. Of course, it was a different kind of duck than back in Austria-Hungary, but they quickly adapted to the local variety."

The evolution of the duck feathered garment craze can be seen in these two pictures, taken in 1878 (left) and 1902 (right). Things got a little out of hand.

By the end of 1875, the Czech tailors had built several shops and homes near the railroad. Even though an official station had yet to be constructed, the train stopped each time it passed through due to the ducks on the tracks. The Czechs would greet the delightfully delayed train riders with new fashionable duck vests and trousers, which became quite the Central Texas rage. Before long, the conductors had grown sick of the smoked duck, and a station was added. People came north, south, east, and west, to have their own duck-feathered garments fitted by the now famous duck tailors.

Other retailers soon set-up shop to provide services to the visitors. Seeing an opportunity, German tailors – who worked mostly in cotton – moved in and began growing their preferred medium. By 1876, the City of Taylorsville was incorporated. They intended the name to advertise the city's primary industry, but the misspelling of "tailor" as "taylor" by the English-learning immigrants led a conductor named Edward Moses Taylor to

Unknown young woman wearing a "fasionable" duck feathered dress, circa 1900. Also unknown if she was wearing it by will or by force.

believe the town was named after him. When the city leaders discovered the error but saw how thrilled ol' Eddie was, they didn't have the heart to tell him it was all a misunderstanding.

Dropping the "Ville"

Since the misspelled name of the town failed to attract business, several companies were forced to save money on their signage and shorten the name of the town to simply "Taylor." The budget records of the Taylor Five-and-Dime, the first to use the shortened name, reflect a savings of $30 (adjusted for inflation) on their new sign in 1879. Other businesses would follow suite, and in 1892 the name was officially truncated to Taylor.

The tailoring industry in Taylor would steadily decline over the next decade as duck feathers went out of style. With the Czech's gimmick no longer pulling in the customers, the German tailors moved on as well. By 1910, the last tailor in Taylor went out of business, and there hasn't been a tailor in Taylor since then. However, their legacy remained as the new king was crowned: cotton.

CHAPTER 2 – COTTON

Though Taylor was founded on the death of ducks, it rose on the cushion of cotton. After the tailors, both Czech and German, no longer did business in the town they so optimistically named, the cotton industry started by the German tailors continued to flourish. By the early 1900s, Taylor was one of the largest in-land exporters of cotton in the nation. In fact, the Taylorians were so surrounded by the stuff, many colloquialisms entered the lexicon to refer to it.

Early Taylor Colloquialisms for Cotton
the soft stuff
ground clouds
Texas snow
that good ol' stuff
puffy stuff
plant hair
white gold
the pillow crop
angel poo
cot cot
plant wool
tailor's delight
field cushion

Early Cotton Developments

There are several factors that contributed to the success of the cotton crops in and around Taylor. The soil had been fertilized by duck droppings for hundreds of years, making it well suited for the taxing growth of cotton. To replenish the nutrients year after year, farmers herded the aquatic fowl over their fields in hopes of netting some droppings. Of course, once the cotton bloomed, farmers struggled to keep the ducks away from the crop. Cleaning duck poop out of cotton bolls was messy business.

While the farmers profited from

exporting cotton, other enterprising locals would attempt to cash in on the cash crop. Greg Benson, a civil engineer from Texas A&M, attempted to utilize cotton as a building material as part of his doctoral studies. In 1908, he built a small house out of only cotton balls, hot glue, and construction paper. It maintained its structure for a day, until a small gust of wind picked it up and a subsequent drizzle reduced it to mush. Afterward, the Taylor Gazette reported that Benson tried to improve the design by experimenting with a wider variety of glue – including Elmer's and Super – and by utilizing sturdier poster board in place of construction paper.

Benson's 2nd cotton house before it was destoryed in a summer hail storm in 1909.

The second attempt still failed to produce the desired results, and he got points deducted when the professor realized it was too good for him to have done on his own and his parents must have helped.

Cotton-Gin

When one hears the term "cotton gin", many think of the invention by Eli Whitney. However, in Taylor, the word took on another meaning altogether. A French immigrant, Jean-Baptiste Brasseur, imported juniper berries – the basis of the alcoholic beverage gin – from an orchard outside of the neighboring town of Thrall. By adding an extraction from cottonseeds and leaves to a traditional gin and soaking it in cotton fibers for a specific period of time, he concocted a new delightful spirit. Brasseur kept his recipe a secret, and thus the so-called cotton-gin would never reach a nationwide market. However, it would be distributed along the railroad that came through town and was the house spirit of the Duck's Back Saloon.

During prohibition in the 1920's, cotton-gin grew particularly popular due to being soaked into cotton and stored in glass jars. A jar of dry cotton and a jar of cotton-gin were difficult to distinguish unless the jar was picked-up (its weight giving it away) or opened for inspection. Luckily, law enforcement couldn't touch such property without a search warrant or probable cause. Often, prohibition violators would keep several decoy jars of dry cotton to decrease the possibility of the cotton-gin being selected to examine if such searches did occur. However, the ruse wouldn't last forever.

Jean-Baptiste Brasseur holding an early jar of cotton-gin, circa 1915. Curtesy of the Brasseur family.

Despite the actions of various secret societies working covertly in the city, in 1927 the Taylor City Council passed an ordinance requiring all cotton to be stored in paper bags. This made the storage of gin-soaked cotton impractical. While Congress repealed the prohibition of alcohol in 1933, Taylor never got around to reversing the paper bag requirement for cotton storage, and thus cotton-gin remained impossible to produce or store legally in the city of its invention. To this day, Taylorians could have any cotton stored in non-paper containers confiscated, along with a $15 fine. Though, the last time this

Jar of illegal cotton-gin found in the home of Mabel Barnet by her family after her death in 1965. It had been sitting on the shelf for over 40 years.

was widely enforced was the mid-1990s, usually only when the police station was low on q-tips.

Cotton-Harvesting Ducks

The harvesting of cotton had always been hard work, and creating a machine to do it was even harder. International Harvester wouldn't produce the first commercially successful cotton picker until 1947. For reference, the first atomic bomb detonation happened two years before that. Yes, harvesting cotton was a tough nut to crack. However, the farmers in early Taylor had one resource that most cotton-growing regions lacked: thousands of ducks just standing around. In 1918, they would be put to use by Colonel J.C. Owens, who returned to his family's farm after serving in World War I.

Though he was laughed at by most locals, Owens held hard to his belief that ducks could be trained to pick cotton better than humans or the various early mechanical contraptions. Below are some excerpts from his journal, detailing his process for cotton-training.

> *"I have begun my second trial for the training of ducks in the harvesting of cotton bolls. This time, I will start training the fowl from birth. The animals have intelligence, so I believe; they have just had no opportunity to demonstrate it to our eyes.*
>
> *"To teach the cotton-picking behavior in the ducklings, I have set up a miniature cotton field, with small bits of cotton attached to twigs. Through experiment, I have discovered the ducks have excellent night vision, allowing them to harvest by moonlight or starlight, for the white cotton glows bright even for human eyes at night. I will show the ducklings that when a bit of cotton is placed in a bright red bin, a breadcrumb will be produced as their reward. I do not see how this could fail, and by the end of the growing season, I expect ducks not only to fertilize our fields, but also to harvest the very crop their droppings helped to prosper."*

Owens with his ducks, circa 1920.

It would take Owens three more trials before he succeeded in training a duck to pick cotton in the harvest of 1920. One night during a full moon, he took a flock of twelve "cotton-pluckers," as he affectionately called them, to a sectioned-off area of his family's cotton crop. By morning, the gaggle had plucked the entire acre. What once had taken 125 man-hours to harvest, Owens had done in eight man-hours and 96 duck-hours – and the ducks worked for breadcrumbs.

It would be three years before the Colonel had trained enough ducks to work his entire crop. For those years, he kept his entire operation a secret. In the spring of 1923, Owens revealed his mastery of cotton to a journalist from Austin, bypassing the local news. The writer was thoroughly amazed and published his story in the Texas Weekly newsletter. Below is an excerpt:

> *"Owen's quackers have perfected cotton-picking to a degree the machine-makers could only dream of. While the sight of the white-feathered fowl waddling down the rows is laughable, in time it will be Owens who will laugh the loudest. Paying hired hands to harvest his crop costs roughly 25% of his proceeds. The cost of the ducks, their food, and their care, reduces that expense to 3%.*
>
> *"He estimates that by 1950, ducks using his patent pending technique will be harvesting half of the world's cotton, and by the year 2000, ducks will be collecting not only all of the world's cotton, but other crops as well."*

The Bread Raid

Despite his high hopes, Owen's dream wouldn't last. After a successful harvest in 1923, he spent the next fall and spring training a new batch of ducks. By the summer, they numbered over two hundred. It was right as the cotton began to bloom that the unthinkable happened. Owen's ducks mutinied and raided the city for bread, which he had so masterfully trained them to crave. It only took them one night. Most residents didn't know they had been looted until they woke to find all bread missing and single bolls of cotton in every red-colored cup or container.

Owens was devastated, and it took weeks for the city's bread supply to be replenished. Now realizing they could get bread themselves, the cotton plucking ducks would never return to the fields. To this day, residents will bring an offering of stale bread to the town's ducks in hopes that the raid will not be repeated. So far, they have been satisfied.

Over the next decades, Taylor's dominance in cotton would gradually wane, supplemented with other crops. But in its history, Taylor will always be ruled by cotton.

CHAPTER 3 – DUCKS

You've already read how ducks led to the founding of Taylor and the success of its agriculture. That is only the start of the town's connection with the animal.

Early Duck Utilization

Paleontologists estimate that ducks have inhabited the Taylor area for at least 10,000 years. In fact, if one digs down more than five feet, the likeliness of finding a fossilized duckbill is surprisingly high.

During the founding years, ducks were in such abundance they were used for every conceivable application. Of course, as mentioned in Chapter 1, the Czech tailors used the feathers for garment making, but they didn't let the rest of the bird go to waste. The meat was incorporated into a variety of dishes - everything from duck jerky to duck quesadillas, or "duck-a-dillas" as the Parrilla Pato (Duck Grill) named the entrée. The Duck-Mattress Company (the original name of Taylor Bedding) was established by Douglas Wolfe in 1877 to make use of the tons of feathers that were too ruffled or damaged to use on garments. The factory not only built mattresses, but also duck-feather pillows and cushions. They were not particularly comfortable or soft, but since they were essentially stuffed with trash, they were very cheap – about a third of the price of other feather-filled sleeping surfaces.

Dig a hole almost anywhere around Taylor, and you'll find some fossilzed duck-bills.

Discarded duckbills became a medium of trade, a pseudo-currency, that Taylorians used from the city's founding until the turn of the century, when inflation made it impractical. It took two bills to buy a loaf of bread in 1895, whereas five years later the price was a hundred-times that. By early 1901, they were considered valueless. This made local investor Wilford Crawford's duck bill fortune – an estimated two million duck bills contained in a fifty-foot silo – essentially worthless. His wife tried decorating them to sell at festival booths, but they would never recover their value. Adjusted for inflation, his collection of duckbills would have amounted to an estimated $50 million at their peak value in 1883. Crawford died penniless in 1904, by diving head first into his half-full silo.

It was then that his wife finally found a way to recoup some of the unwise investment. She sold tickets for people to witness the silo being blown up by dynamite. She got the idea from a similar spectacle, known as the Crash at Crush, held a few years earlier. At that event, forty thousand people came to watch two steam locomotives crash at full speed. Unexpectedly to the organizers, but perhaps not surprising to you or me, the crash caused an explosion that resulted in many injuries and a few fatalities. Ms. Crawford promised that better safety measures would be in place at the "Duckbill Dynamiting," as it was advertised. The event got attention state wide and allowed the Czech tailors to promote their going-out-of-style duck-feathered garments one last time. In the end, the explosion was reported as a success, with only five injuries from duckbill impaling.

No cameras were present at the Duck-Bill Dynamiting, but an unknown Taylorian artist "did their best."

The Great Goose Invasion

Throughout the decades, the duck population would steadily decrease, but never disappear entirely. Geese eventually conquered the town's largest lake at Murphy Park, pushing most ducks to the smaller pond at Bull Branch. In the 1970's, the City Council attempted to evict the pesky geese from the lake and restore its rightful duck residents. As anyone who has dealt with geese can guess, the sheriff and his deputies were unsuccessful. Three officers were hospitalized, and the rest suffered post-traumatic episodes whenever they heard a squawk. Thus, the council had no choice but to approve a treaty granting the geese domain over the park's lake. They, at times, allow duck visitations, but claim any bread that residents bring to their waters.

Unknown officer unsuccesfully attempts to evict geese from City Lake.

The Mascot

Of course, most central Texas citizens know the duck as the mascot of Taylor schools and sports teams. Surprisingly, this was not always the case. The use of mascots for schools did not become popular until sometime in the early 1900s. Even then, the duck seemed like a natural fit, but "Taylor Duck" did not roll off the tongue, in the school board's opinion. As schools began to have mascots, most used alliteration in their town and mascot names, such as the Hutto Hippos, Granger Grasshoppers, and the Thrall Thrigers. Taylor's School Board decided to follow the trend and be known as the "Taylor Termites".

The costumed Termy the Termite at a Taylor Termite football game, circa 1923. Student unknown, as they should be.

On the sidelines during football games, a termite-infested block of wood served as a living mascot. This practice was abandoned after the termites escaped and settled in the wooden high-rise bleachers. In 1919, they covertly feasted from December to August. During the first home game that year, the stands collapsed. Although nobody was seriously injured, the team did lose the game, and for the rest of the year the fans had to sit in lawn chairs.

Even this disaster did not initiate the switch from Termite to Duck. However, it did result in a costumed mascot replacing the living termites. Serving as Termy Taylor the Taylor Termite was considered a high honor, but the student often suffered from dental problems due to constantly gnawing on the block of wood during games.

Taylor ducks making sure the Taylor Ducks became the Taylor Ducks.

The Duck, specifically the mallard, became Taylor schools' official mascot in 1938. The year was particularly dry, and the bog outside the neigh-boring town of Hutto nearly dried up. The hippo population became restless and began to wander away from the wetlands they had inhabited since escaping from a passing circus train twenty years earlier. The ducks did not appreciate the large mammals taking up residence in their dwindling creeks and streams (the lakes in Taylor had yet to be built). Although the white-feathered ducks were too afraid to take action, the mallards formed attack flocks. In a coordinated effort, they swarmed the imposing beasts, forcing them out of the waters of Taylor, and chased them north to the Granger area. A den of lions, who had also escaped from a passing circus train – they were notoriously insecure at the time – attacked and killed the hippos. This event also led Granger to change its mascot from the grasshopper to the lion. Hutto remained the hippos, despite the striking lack of hippos in the town afterward. The lions of Granger still roam the outskirts of town near the train tracks. Don't venture there alone!

Now convinced of the ferocity and strength of the duck, the school board unanimously voted to change the mascot to the animal most associated with the town's culture.

CHAPTER 4 – TAYLOR SCHOOLS

Since its founding, Taylor schools have been highly spirited and prideful, though at times mediocre. The first schools were started by the immigrant populations, Czech, German, Swedish, and the one Polish guy, as was common in western settlements. This kept the ethnic groups mostly segregated, not only in their education, but also in their social lives. It was as if multiple towns occupied the same space with little interaction. The taboo of a German and Czech dating or marrying each other lingered until nearly the turn of the century.

Integrations

It wasn't until 1893, seventeen years after the founding of the town, that the first integrated English-language public school opened its doors. As the immigrants united around a common education and language, their social lives began to mix. Over the following decades, this would result in an intermingling of genes that would leave few ethnically pure individuals of European decent being born by the 1920s. Of course, while segregation along the European ethnicities began to vanish, segregation along racial lines remained. African-American and most Hispanic students attended separate schools until the late 1960s. It's a shame that while we had the technology to put a man on the Moon, we hadn't the wisdom to realize that everyone deserves to be treated as equals.

Taylor School Sports

Sports have long been a strong part of Taylor schools, though few state championships have been earned. In 1982, the Taylor Ice Hockey team made a magical run through the state playoffs thanks to three large families that moved in from Canada. There were only a dozen other teams in the state, and most practiced on roller skates. The team disbanded when the Canadians left town and only two remaining players had ever seen an ice rink. One of those students was a second cousin of Emilio Estevez, of *Mighty Ducks* fame. The actor has steadfastly denied there's any connection between the Taylor Ducks and the Mighty Ducks, but he's fooling no one.

Football is king in Texas, and Taylor bends knee to the crown. The first Taylor Football team, back when the Termite was still the mascot, didn't fare well. They were undersized and constantly gnawed on their wooden mouthpieces. Their first win came against a Thorndale Bulldog team that had been struck by food poisoning after eating at a local restaurant before the game. The coach suspected the chocolate pie they had eaten for dessert. All but three of the bulldogs had to sit out the second half. Taylor eked out a win 14 to 13.

After the mascot was changed to the Duck, they seemingly fared better. During one especially rainy fall, the team was undefeated halfway through the season. Every game so far that year had been played in the rain, but the Farmer's Almanac forecasted a dry November and December. To combat the situation, Coach Drake Mallard had a sprinkler system installed to simulate rainfall during the rest of the home games that year.

A visiting Round Rock Dragons team tried to protest, as the water seemed to extinguish their fire, but the officials could find no rule prohibiting the strategy. The wet Ducks easily toppled the cooled off Dragons. But, they would fall short when the Rockdale Tigers spiked the

Game time in Taylor with the sprinklers sprinkling.

sprinklers with herbicides the week before their annual meeting. By Friday night, the grass had died, and while the ducks played well in the rain, Coach Mallard knew that they would not fare as well as the Tigers in the mud. The ducks were forced to play without their sprinklers to avoid creating a mud pit, and thus lost the game by a wide margin. By the next year, the state had banned the use of sprinklers during games, and the team would return to mediocrity.

Academic Decathlon

While sports championships have proved rare for Taylor, academic championships have been plentiful. The highly successful Taylor High School Academic Decathlon team saw its start in the 1998-1999 school year. The charter team made it to the small school state finals and missed placing third by seven points, which amounts to less than one question on any of the dozens of tests that were taken by the team's members. "SEVEN POINTS" became the battle cry the team still calls before testing, though the meaning has been lost on the team's current members.

The only reason the origin is known and included in this account is that your author, Andrew Morris, was a member of that charter team in the late 90's. Another member, Bobby Leshikar, would later return to Taylor as an English teacher and Language Arts department chair at Taylor High School for several years in the 2010s. But, while a student, the team would scratch Leshikar's beard – grown since middle school – before every event. However, Leshikar was a senior, thus next year's team would be unable to continue the tradition. To solve the problem, Leshikar's beard was ritualistically shaved (against his will) by the underclassmen after graduation. The hair was collected and traveled with the team for good luck.

This work of art, titled "Taking Bobby's Beard" was first displayed in the 1999 Taylor High School Art Exhibition. Artist unknown.

Mr. Leshikar, after returning to Taylor High School as a teacher, made many attempts to steal his precious beard back from the team – and occasionally succeeded. However, following each successful liberation, the team launched a counterassault to recover the legendary facial hair.

Upon learning that Leshikar would be leaving his teaching position at the end of the 2017 school year, the team decided that the beard belonged with its rightful owner. They presented it to him on the last day of school and gave it one last scratch.

Taylor High School Band

Leshikar and yours truly also served the school as drum majors in the Taylor High School Marching Band in the late 1990s. This coincided with a revival of the band program at Taylor High School, though we were not the ones responsible. A new band director, known only as Rubio, would lead the band to UIL Division 1 ratings across both marching and concert band competitions for the first time in decades. A tall dark Spaniard with long flowing hair, Rubio both intimidated and inspired all who received his instruction.

Rubio gazing upon his Creation.

During Rubio's reign, the band size would increase from around forty students to over a hundred. Half-time shows went from embarrassing to exceptional. New sleek modern uniforms replaced frilly 80's style garb. The membership shifted from mostly social outcasts to a diverse mixture of individuals from all parts of the student body. There wasn't a student who didn't respect, fear, and love Rubio. From the heat of summer band practices to the coldest December playoff games, Rubio would keep his band focused and motivated. Later directors would continue the trend after the mysterious departure of Rubio. Through the years, the band only became more dedicated. The size would cycle up and down due to purges of unworthy members every two to four years, necessary to maintain the high level of commitment expected. However, since

Rubio established the high expectations, the quality of the Taylor High School Band has rarely wavered.

Taylor Campuses

It is often said, or perhaps this is the first time, that a school is not just the students and staff, but the building as well. Several existing buildings in town have served as Taylor High School in the past. The oldest still standing is located on 7th Street and has recently become an interesting destination. Supposedly some businesses have worked their way inside, despite the current owner's best efforts to seal-up the cracks around the doors and windows.

Side-entrance of the Old Taylor High, before all the businesses found their way in.

The building was constructed in 1923, and so is nearly upon its 100th year. On that fateful day, a time capsule planted during its construction is scheduled to be unearthed. *(Those reading this after 2023, please change all verb tenses to past).* Inside is said to be a copy of the Taylor Daily Press, a photo of the school board members, a duckbill, a signed roster of that year's Taylor Termites football team, and a bottle of cotton-gin donated by the Duck's Back Saloon. It is the only known remaining bottle of the locally created spirit after the recipe died with its inventor. Liquor experts estimate its value in the five figures. Already, collectors are circling the date on their calendars.

The New Taylor High School was built in 1969, and in an effort to end racially identifiable schools and lingering voluntary segregation, the district would begin an unwritten policy that has lasted even to today. For the first time, all students in the city in a specific grade would attend the same school. This resulted in unifying the town across all lines. There would not be boundary disputes or inequality of access. It has caused some problems, though. Transportation would be simpler if Taylor had several neighborhood Kindergarten-through-5th-Grade elementary schools, instead of having several elementary schools with only 2 or 3 grade levels each. (In fact, by the time you read this, Taylor might have already made the transitioned to that more common arrangement.) But in the current situation, sometimes families with four or five children – distributed every 3 or 4 years – end up with all their kids attending different schools. A parent who wishes to pick up their kids instead of having them ride the bus might take two hours to make the rounds. There are several brave souls who make the run to every school. The "Car Line Queens" (as they call themselves) dart from TH Johnson Elementary, to Pasemann Elementary, to Main Street Intermediate, to Taylor Middle School, and end at Taylor High School. It's not an easy feat, but during the 2018-2019 school year, there were at least four moms and one dad who relentlessly made the trek every school day. One actually had to make a sixth stop at the Legacy Early College campus. By the end of October, three of the Queens had dropped out and decided to throw their older kids on the bus.

Of all the old school buildings, only one was destroyed by accident. The 12th Street School served as a neighborhood elementary school before the opening of TH Johnson Elementary. As part of an end-of-year event during its last year of operation, science teacher William Nigel arranged for the school to break the world record for the largest baking soda and vinegar volcano. Every student brought a large box of Arm & Hammer and a jug of white distilled vinegar. The Piggly-Wiggly had to make a special order to restock their shelves. The volcano was constructed out of paper mâché in the foyer. It stood 8 feet high and stretched fifteen feet wide at the base. Nigel had rigged a mechanism to slowly combine the reactants, but it malfunctioned. Instead of mixing the vinegar and baking soda gradually to produce an oozing, spurting volcano, all two hundred gallons of liquid and five hundred pounds of powder were combined at once. The explosion resulted in no deaths, but the building was filled floor to ceiling with foam, eventually gushing out of the third-floor windows. Even after a summer of cleaning, the vinegar smell could not be tamed. Converting it to a YMCA as planned wouldn't be possible. It was later imploded using an even more violent chemical reaction: dynamite.

Refitting old school buildings is somewhat of a tradition in Taylor.

The gym teacher was able to take this picture after the vinegar-baking soda incident.

The old old high school became the middle school, before the new middle school was built on the Loop. The newer old high school became a 4th-5th grade intermediate campus . . . and several other things. Even the old Northside Elementary became the new behavioral alternative school. The school board is already planning what to convert the new new high school (built in 2012) to when it is eventually retired in the 2050's.

The New New High School

The new new high school has some mystery surrounding its construction. For one, it was finished under budget and on schedule. This would be suspicious enough. However, Harvey Melbourne, the lead contractor, went missing after its completion. Also, throughout the years, exploring students have discovered hidden passages and false walls. Putting it together, some claim that Melbourne now inhabits the school, keeping to the passages and hiding spots he built into it. After investigating, it was uncovered that Harvey Melbourne changed his name from Albert Benson, the name of a graduate of Taylor High School in 1985. Benson had been a popular student: football star running back, salutatorian, and voted most likely to succeed. However, during the first year of college at the University of Houston, he faltered. As a running back, he couldn't gain a positive yard. His grade-point average rarely broke 2.5, and he never landed a single date. He yearned for his glory days in high school. There is no record of him after college until 2005 when he changed his name from Benson to Melbourne and went into construction. Curiously, the only jobs he worked on were high schools. Analyzing the patterns showed that each school construction was completed closer and closer to budget and more and more on time – presumably with an increasing number of hidden passages. How or why Melbourne is able to achieve the former while managing the latter is not known. However, it is known that the new new Taylor High School has secrets yet to be discovered.

The New New Taylor High, featuring 21st Century slanted-roof technology!

The schools of Taylor have always been in integral part of the community, shaping its future residents and representing it on the sports field, testing room, concert hall, and auditorium stage. But, there is more to the town than its agriculture, animal life, and educational system, as the next chapters will show.

CHAPTER 5 – LAKE DRIVE

Lake Drive is the primary residential street in Taylor. It features some of Taylor's largest and most valuable homes and, of course, has a lake. If there were a Taylor-opoloy, it would probably be Park Place. The residential street runs west to east all the way across town with only one stop sign and one stop light, and *no school zones!*

Early Development

Most residents are unaware the original name of the street was Lovers Lane. At the time they paved it in the 1930s, it was the most northern road running east to west across town. Many wealthy Taylorians built large homes on Lovers, and an influx of rich Russians also settled on the west end of the pleasant road on the outskirts of town.

The largest estate, known by some as the Clark Mansion, was home to a dignitary from Moscow. Vlad Solvalock never socialized with locals, which led to rumors and mystery surrounding him and his grounds. For one thing, ducks avoided his property and the small ponds he built on it. Some claimed to spot a sort-of-aquatic rodent, possibly a water-going ferret known as a snipe, darting through the tall grass and slipping in and out of the ponds. Late one night, a den of local cub scouts attempted to trap a snipe using pillow sacks and a special call, but they were unsuccessful.

The street was renamed in the 1950s. During a low duck population season, a family of beavers built a dam on one of the creeks meandering through town. The low Lover's Lane bridge over the small waterway was flooded when the creek backed-up and formed Taylor's first lake. The residents of the Lover's Lane, long tired of the winks and giggles they received when giving their address, saw it as a blessing in disguise. They used the event to petition the street be renamed "Lake Drive", since it now literally featured a drive through a lake. The huge new lake helped the duck population recover, and the dam built by the beavers still stands today. They did impressive rebar and concrete work.

The Island

When it first formed, the lake was without its characteristic central island. A voluntarily homeless citizen, Robert Ronald, built it in the 1960s. Most knew him as "the Collector." Whenever residents put something on the curb, such as an old recliner or chest-of-drawers, it would be gone within hours. Nobody knows how, but without fail the old man would drag the junk out to the center of the lake and add it to his makeshift island. When the collector went missing one day, the island naturally filled with mud and formed a mound in the shallow lake.

Since that time, Collector's Island has been used for various shady deeds. During a heist of City National Bank of Taylor in 1973, the loot was hastily stashed on the island, until a resident discovered it three days later when attempting to dump an unwanted cat. During

Taylorian Cleever Sacowitz sketched this picture of Collector's Island in 1970 while in 2nd grade. The majority of its growth since then can be attributed to egret droppings.

the satanic-cult craze of the 1980s, the island was used by satanists to sacrifice chickens and goats. As you might expect, the City Council would not allow that to continue . . . without a permit.

Collector's Island was also the launch point for the annual 4th of July fireworks display starting in 1985. However, an accident in 1991 caused the complete destruction of the island. No people were seriously injured, and the crew enjoyed the roasted duck that resulted. The local Freemasons rebuilt the island before the next year's show, perhaps for their own motives. There are those that say the seasonal egret infestation was arranged to protect the islands secrets. Stay tuned for more about the island in last chapter!

Christmas Lights

Lake Drive was also the site of the largest coordinated Christmas light display in the history of Taylor. From Debus Street on the west end all the way to the lake on the east, every home participated. It started in 1994. One of Lake Drive's residents, Connor Blue, was frustrated over his eight-year-old son's color blindness. Every Christmas, when the colorful lights would go up, his son would only see white. He decided to coordinate a display that would show everyone how his son saw Christmas, so everybody could be equally depressed by it. Blue went to every house on the street and offered strands of plain white lights and even constructed PVC-pipe arches for every driveway. By the time he was done, the two-mile stretch was completely lined with white lights: not a single color. It was the most beautifully plain, depressingly inspiring Christmas attraction in Texas. After the first year or two, some homes began to abandon the tradition. Blue moved from Taylor in the early 2000s, but in recent years some have tried to bring the tradition back, much to the chagrin of the lazier Lake Drive residents. It's not hard to tell which ones they are.

In the end, Lake Drive personifies Taylor. It will always be the street we try to direct visitors down to avoid the sore spots on a steadily improving 2nd Street. However, for the small businesses of Taylor, downtown is the place to be.

CHAPTER 7 – DOWNTOWN

Downtown Taylor was once the heart of the town, and it is on the verge of regaining that title. To some, it more resembles the human appendix: a left-over part from a previous age that pretty much only causes problems and wouldn't be missed if removed. To others, it is a regrowing bud on torched ground, already springing forward.

In Taylor's early days, as with most small Texas towns, downtown provided citizens' everyday needs. In fact, it was just considered "town." There have been several revival efforts through the last decade, but downtown will probably never return to the glory days of the early 1900's.

Duck's Back Saloon

It was downtown where the Duck's Back Saloon served up its famous cotton-gin. The locally produced spirit brought in customers from all over central Texas. Gregory Tannery, the owner from 1910 to its closing in 1931, became somewhat of a deranged millionaire. Though the saloon brought in hundreds of thousands of dollars a year, even during prohibition, he remained a bachelor in the apartment on the second story of the building. Tannery was rarely seen outside his business, and when seen, never talked to anyone. He would receive shipments from unknown senders several times a month. The unadorned crates would be brought to his upstairs door in the back alley, the contents never seen. When questioned by curious patrons, he would simply say, "Mind your business and I'll mind mine." Then one day, in 1931, Tannery disappeared completely. No one knew if he left town, was kidnapped, or just walked away and died somewhere like an old dog, but his body was never found. With

The large duck stationed atop the Duck's Back Saloon looking over downtown, circa 1930.

no living heirs and no will produced, the Duck's Back was confiscated by the city and turned into the first DMV. At least, that's how the official story goes.

Tannery's fate would remain a mystery until 1976, and has not been published until now. Through a series of anonymous interviews, corroborated by official records, I have pieced together the discovery of Tannery's bunker, perhaps the most successful government cover-up in Williamson County history.

A vertical shaft running deep underground was found during the installation of underground cables in August of 1976. When brought to the attention of city officials, the installer's permits were revoked, and they were run out of town. Jon Davies, the city manager, knew the reported location of the shaft to be where the Duck's Back Saloon once was, and he had long pondered about Tannery's weird dealings. He had been told the story of the disappearance many times; for it happened the same day he was born. Davies thought there must have been a connection between the missing man and this tunnel.

Davies first tried to descend the shaft himself, but found it too unstable for an amateur. He contacted several professional tunneliers from as far away as Dallas. One brave team took up the offer. Joe

Kelly and Rob Slydel of Georgetown, who had mapped much of Inner Space Caverns, were able to reinforce the shaft walls and safely descend.

At the bottom of the shaft, they discovered the remains of an elevator system Tannery used to ascend and descend it. It was remarkably advanced for its time, being driven by a hydraulic lift. That was just the start. If reports are to be believed, Tannery's inventions deep beneath downtown Taylor might have jumpstarted the mechanical and technological revolutions of the 1930's and 40's. In the bunker, they found designs and prototypes of jet and rocket engines, electronic computers, and even a crude jukebox. In addition to the things he had actually built, his journals were filled with even more advanced ideas.

Son of spelunker Joe Kelly says his dad found designs for this contraption in the bunker. They could never figure out what it was.

Tannery's decomposed body was there as well, with copies of letters he sent to various companies and universities detailing his designs and discoveries. But then, one might ask, why the cover up? The discovery that a Taylorian made such advances would surely be cause of celebration and pride! Well, it had to do with where those letters were sent. All were addressed to locations in Germany.

Tannery was a child of a German tailor who settled in Taylor shortly after its founding. During World War I, Tannery, of course, publicly claimed to support the United States and its Allies against his parent's home country, and perhaps he did. But after the Great War, his pride in his heritage seemingly resumed. We may never know why, but in secret he began to use all of his profit from the Duck's Back to fund his underground enterprise for Germany's benefit. It is likely that Tannery's rocket designs gave German engineers a five-year head start leading up to World War II.

Even though Tannery was dead before the Nazi party took power in 1933, and perhaps Tannery would have opposed their heinous actions before and during the war, Davies still considered it a treasonous discovery. He paid for the spelunkers' silence with jars of cotton-gin found in the bunker. But, at least one more person would have to be sworn to secrecy: the demolitionist he hired to blow up the bunker and everything in it. Luckily, he knew one he could trust. A friend from college, Pablo Alderete, lined the bunker with dynamite and destroyed all evidence of Taylor's secret skunkworks, except for a single photograph he took before leaving. On May 4th, 1976, the Taylor Daily Press reported that some residents, mostly near downtown, felt a small earthquake. Seismologists at the time had no explanation.

Tannery had one more secret that not even Davies would learn, but which now has finally come to light. While setting the demolition charges, Alderete came across a note that Davies had missed: Tannery's suicide note. Its revelation would be too crushing for Alderete to reveal his old friend. The reason that Tannery locked himself in his bunker to die: his son had been born *that* day –.

This is the only known photo from inside Tannery's bunker, taken by the demolitionist before destroying it.

Tannery wrote that watching his son raised by another man would slowly kill him. He figured it would be better to die in the darkness than live watching that happen, and he couldn't risk the shame that would come to the mother if anyone ever found out. Alderete recognized the date on the letter as Jon Davies' birthday. For, Jon Davies, the city manager, was Gregory Tannery's only son.

The Howard Theatre

For every Gregory Tannery there would be a Griffin Howard – there was exactly one of each. Howard, as you may guess, founded the Howard Theatre in 1914 – the year World War I broke out. Howard was a patriot in all respects. If not for his bad knee, he would have proudly been on the ground in Europe. The Howard Theatre would open to show wartime documentaries and news film. With the upstairs theatre then open as a balcony, it was the largest theatre in Williamson county.

When the War was over, the theatre would transition to showing Hollywood's products. The big stars of Los Angeles would grace the Taylor screen for the next few decades, only pausing when Griffin Howard died in 1941. The Howard estate would finally sell the property in 1974, with a binding stipulation that it would always remain "The Howard Theatre" and never be redeveloped as any other form of business. Finding lasting success proved difficult. Going through several owners over the next few decades, the theatre opened and closed sporadically. Most Taylorians would lose track of whether it was in business or not. The most recent owners found some stability showing first-run movies with competitive ticket prices and a value on concessions; however, the covid shutdown seems to have put an end to that. It

The Howard Theatre, currently with nothing showing.

shutdown with the rest of the movie theaters, but unlike the others, has not reopened.

City National Bank

And what would downtown be without a few financial institutions? The greatest in Taylor is City National Bank. Despite the oxymoronic name, City National is Taylor's most popular and trusted bank. They have well over three ATMs spread across town and several staffed locations – some of which are open after 3pm!

The "motor bank", which originally drove around town so customers could make deposits and withdrawals from their doorsteps, broke down in the late 80s and has since remained at the corner of 3rd and Vance. The wheels were taken off and the pneumatic tubes, which before had reached out like translucent spider legs to customers' front doors and windows, now simply dropped down next to their cars. On paydays for much of the 1990s, cars filled all five lanes up to six cars deep. Alas, with the development of the internet, mobile banking apps, and direct deposit, customers can once again make deposits from home. However, taking a picture of a check with your phone can't compare to the fun we had watching that cylindrical canister magically shoot through those clear pneumatic tubes.

Though downtown Taylor has had its ups and downs, it seems to be on the upswing in recent years. More shops and restaurants are

The motor bank was bricked into place after the wheels were removed. The pneumatic tubes are now locked in place as well.

opening – and staying open. Of the older establishments, Taylor Sporting Goods has become a landmark, and the world-famous Louie Mueller BBQ is as good as ever. The newly established Texas Beer Company has become the most popular bar since the Duck's Back Saloon. There's no doubt: Taylor wouldn't be Taylor without downtown.

CHAPTER 7 – OTHER TAYLOR BUSINESSES

Throughout its history, there have been many locally owned businesses and restaurants (which are a kind of business) that have helped shape the culture of Taylor. From the very first tailor shops opened by the founding Czechs and Germans to the new hipster coffee shops that appear and disappear mysteriously, Taylor's history teems with an enterprising spirit. Many have already been mentioned. This chapter covers a few more that deserve recognition.

New Orleans Shave Ice

Some successful businesses arise to serve a need that wasn't being met; others create a need that people didn't know they had, and probably didn't need either. Jeffory Dufresne (pronounced Doo-FRAYN) is an example of the latter. Dufresne originated from New Orleans, riding into Taylor on his last dime in 1934. He took a job at Wayne's Appliances, "*the town's only seller of iceboxes and other modern conveniences*" (which was their tagline). As you probably know, iceboxes were not electrically cooled, but instead stocked with blocks of ice to keep their contents

New Orleans Shave Ice, circa 2015

chilled. Taylorians purchased this ice from another business in town: Mr. Freeze's Hard Water Blocks.

After a few days on the job at Wayne's, Dufresne was sent to Mr. Freeze's to get some blocks of ice for the demo iceboxes on display in the store. He noticed that the blocks sold by Mr. Freeze's were a bit too tall and wide for the newest model icebox that had just come in. These iceboxes were better insulated and thus required less ice. Dufresne had to shave about an 1/8 of an inch off the top and the side for it to fit. Instead of alerting Mr. Freeze's about the incompatibility , Dufresne decided to take matters into his own hands and make a little money on the side. Upon selling one of the new iceboxes, Dufresne gave a coupon offering four free ice-block shavings, and 10% off the next five. All the customer needed to do after picking up a block from Mr. Freeze was to swing by Wayne's and Dufresne would shave the ice down to size.

Dufresne shaving an ice block down to size.

You might see where this is going. By going beyond simply shaving the ice and letting it go to waste, Dufresne's idea would launch a completely new product. The story goes that two weeks into his ice-shaving scheme, a mother and her boy came into Wayne's carrying a block of ice for Dufresne to shave. It was a hot July day, and the boy was so thirsty he nearly started licking the ice-block as Dufresne began to shave it. Seeing the boy's anguish, Dufresne fetched a cup and shaved some of the ice into it. The boy quickly consumed it and begged for another, despite the mother's hushes. Dufresne pandered to the boy, this time even squeezing in some juice from an orange he had peeled for a snack.

The rest, as they say, is history. Dufresne's first New Orleans Shave Ice stand started as a table outside the 12th Street Elementary School that August when school started session. He had spent weeks developing a mechanical-crank ice-shaver that could make ten cups of shaved-ice in one minute. He had also developed several flavorings: orange, lemon, peach, and tiger's-blood – imported directly from India. These flavorings were not as thick and sweet as the syrups used today; they were little more than juice with a little extra sugar added. The only exception was the tiger's-blood, which was served natural. Quickly congealing, it produced a gummy texture kids loved, as long as they finished before scabs formed.

A real tiger's blood shave ice was not for the faint of heart.

Dufresne started selling his shave-ice for ten cents a cup. After quickly going through his ice block each of the first three days, he rose the price to an entire quarter. The children didn't care. They would do anything to be one of the lucky ones that got the cold treat. Dufresne would eventually build a small stand on the newly paved Lover's Lane (later renamed Lake Drive) on the northern outskirts of town. He would stay open later to attract the teenagers and older folks as they went for evening drives. His stand became a must-stop on any Taylor date-night. Dufresne would eventually sell the business and move back to New Orleans, and the stand would go through several rebuilds and upgrades through the decades. For a while in the late 80's, after a few mild summers, shave-ice sales dropped, and the stand converted into a film-drop-off booth. But after converting back to shave-ice in the mid-90s, it's been the go-to cold-treat stand in town, featuring many more flavors. As you may guess, the "tiger's-blood" flavor no longer contains any actual tiger blood (due to endangered species protections). Locally sourced bobcat blood is used as a substitute.

Taylor Meat Company

Ice is nice, but meat is better. For that, there is Taylor Meat Company. Started as a butcher shop in downtown Taylor in the mid-1900s, they have since moved to a large facility near the overpass on Highway 79. The founders, instead of using their own last name for the company, decided to use the "where-we-are-and-what-we-sell" naming strategy, to much success. The company is most loved by the locals for their red hotdog wieners, which are sold under the "Tip-Top" brand in stores. While packages now are adorned with a spinning top logo, the original design featured a humanlike pig in formal attire, including a cane and top hat. While most pay the old logo no mind, the origin was worth investigating.

It seems as though 'Tip-Top" wasn't the only brand name the company had considered, although the other options they considered all seemed to revolve around the same theme: Fancy Pants, Posh Pig, and Coat & Tie Cuts, to name a few. When Tip-Top was chosen, the company went all-in. All employees (mostly family members of the founders) were required to be in tip-top formal attire when on the job. They also spoke with terrible posh British accents. During the 50's while still located downtown, it wasn't unusual to see a butcher on his break walking down Main in a tuxedo splashed with the blood of various animals. One particular butcher, Clarence Nolton, was known for commenting to everyone he passed, "I sure hate wearing this bloody coat and bow-tie all day," with a bad Cockney accent. The pun got few laughs but his own. By the 1970's, upon their move to the new facility, the formal attire gimmick had run its course, and they started dressing like hippies instead.

Of course, the real thing you want to know about Taylor Meat is how they make the famous red hotdog weiners. The answer, again: bobcat blood.

Video Station

One of the most unique businesses now in Taylor opened in the mid-90s as rather ordinary establishment. There were at least two other video rental locations in Taylor when Video Station was built. But, the video rental industry has gone through drastic changes in the last 25 years. Netflix started offering DVD rentals by mail for a flat-rate monthly fee in 1999. Later, its move to video streaming would make it responsible for more internet traffic than any other website. In the mid-2000's, Redbox automated the video rental experience with self-serve kiosks. Now, instead of meandering around a store looking for a movie, one just stands and stares at a screen.

Somehow, Video Station has managed to survive these changes. Blockbusters and Hollywood Videos have shut their doors, but the

Inside Video Station, circa 2020. It's all still there!

independently owned and operated Video Station somehow maintains its existence. But how? Some say their vast VHS library brings in technologically nostalgic customers from all over central Texas. Perhaps the recent resurging love for the simpler times of the 80s and 90s has people seeking out the rows and rows of tapes and discs instead of the endless scrolling Netflix suggestions. Maybe there is a satisfaction that comes with making a choice by selecting a physical object to take home. It could be the excitement of holding a movie in each hand, comparing the synopses on the back, and knowing that for good or ill, once you commit there is no going back. There is definitely something keeping the establishment afloat when all other ships have sunk. But can video rentals, along with the various other items for sale in the aisles, really account for it all?

Like in all cases in my research for this book, I decided to investigate. It would take some courage. I hadn't been inside the store in well over a decade. There was some primal fear keeping me from entering. Perhaps it was PTSD from a $132 overdue rental charge I had back in 2001. But, with my wife's help, I was eventually able to venture inside. The nostalgia trip was intense. The same genre signage crowned the aisles. The hundreds – nay – thousands of VHS tapes still lined the shelves. I think it was when I spotted the six DVD copies of *Jingle All the Way* that I started to question reality. This place was an impossible place. It shouldn't be here. Not in this time, not in this place. It belongs in the late 20th century and the first decade of the 21st, or in some hipster urban area. How is it here?! How is it in Taylor. Freaking. Texas?

My wife and the storeowner must have sensed my loosening grasp on sanity. Finally, I snapped and shouted, "Seventeen copies of the movie *Stealth* shouldn't even exist in this world!", as I tore through the aisles. They pursued me. The more I saw, the further from the real world I drifted. Multiple VHS copies of 1993's *Surf Ninjas* starring Rob Schneider can't be sitting there on a shelf available to rent in Taylor, Texas, in the year 2021. It just cannot be so, my logical mind told me. But it was so, and the paradox continued to bleed my mind until my pursuers finally caught me and force-fed me some CDB gummies.

"Oh," I said as the calming chemicals hit my brain, "now it all makes sense."

The prophesy goes that if the last copy of Stealth is rented, the world ends.

CHAPTER 8 – FORGOTTEN HERO OF TAYLOR

Throughout Taylor history, there have been several individuals that rose above the rest to achieve fame at some level beyond the city limits. There was a Texas governor, a Hollywood actor/alcoholic, a famous rodeo cowboy, and even the creator of an animated rabbit. Most Taylorians already know of these, so they are not included in this volume. Instead, this will focus on one that has achieved fame, though has gone unrecognized in the community that brought him forth.

Wilbur the Pig

The 1995 film *Babe* holds a special place in the childhoods of many 80's and 90's kids. It would teach us lessons, like we're all murders for eating meat, and it's fine to break the spirit of the rules as long as the letter of the law is followed. Plus, its famous quote "That'll do, pig" is fun to belittle people with.

And none of that would be, if not for Wilbur the Pig. In the early 90s, the future pig star was given as a gift to a family that lived in the country outside of Taylor. The family named him after the pig in *Charlottes Web*, unaware he was a rare breed of talking pig. Of course, talking pigs are not aware of the meaning of what they say; that would be absurd. But, like parrots, talking pigs may develop associations between simple words and objects or actions, but they cannot construct meaningful sentences or understand complex grammar. For instance, they constantly mix up *their*, *there*, and *they're*, and end almost every sentence with a preposition. And you can completely give up on them getting *its* and *it's* straight. But, talking pigs do have a knack for repeating what they hear or read word-for-word, which makes them as good or better than most actors.

Wilbur would make his way to Hollywood in 1994. The family, who remained anonymous, started him out with commercials. But, it seemed the only auditions he could get were for bacon, pork chops, and other pig-related food products. The family thought that was a tad too morbid. They held out until the perfect role came up, and luckily it soon did.

The movie was titled *Gordy*, and Wilbur ended up auditioning against a non-talking pig for the lead role. They thought he would be a shoe-in. However, Wilbur froze-up at the audition. Instead of reciting the lines they had rehearsed, he would just say "oink" – by which I mean he would pronounce the word "oink" over and over again, not actually make the natural oinking sound of a pig.

The family was devastated. How long would they have to wait for another movie starring a pig in the lead role? Not long, as it turned out. Pigs were all the range in the mid-90s, so it would seem. Another pig-oriented movie titled *Babe* started auditions the following week, with a pig – again – starring in the titular role. This time, Wilbur recited his lines perfectly and even bantered a bit with James Cromwell, even asking him "aren't you that guy from that movie?"

Babe was an astounding success, but that had not been a guarantee. *Gordy,* which was released only 3 months earlier, had completely flopped. Seeing those poor box office results for another movie starring a pig put everyone at the studio on pins and needles. *Babe* had cost $30 million to produce, and *Gordy* took in only four million at the box office. Even if *Babe* sold twice the tickets *Gordy* had, it would still be a major loss for the studio. But, *Babe* had something *Gordy* didn't: a real talking pig . . . and James Cromwell.

Wilbur in the lime-light.

Babe would earn over $200 million worldwide, be nominated for Best Picture, and even spawn a sequel a few years later. Wilbur would not star in the sequel, *Babe: Pig in the City*, as he had grown too big by then. Without Wilbur, the sequel didn't make even half of its budget back. It would be the origin of the Hollywood saying, "If you want the pig to talk, then get a talking pig," which means to cast the actor that has the characteristics of the character they will portray, instead of trying to give the actor the needed characteristics using special effects or training.

The success wouldn't change Wilbur's family. Even though they were now rich from the royalties from the movie, they maintained their anonymity. They returned to Taylor immediately after filming on *Babe* had wrapped, and never revealed the movie star to other locals. In fact, they didn't announce anything to the public until his death in 2003. They held a memorial, but not on their property in order to keep their identities secret. Several Hollywood elites, James Cromwell, and the younger talking-dog from *Homeward Bound* were in attendance. Babe held a special place in the hearts of hundreds of others who came to pay their respects. Some claimed the movie had made them vegetarians – if only for a few days. Even though he wasn't a person, Wilbur was by far the most famous Taylorian.

That'll do, pig. That'll do . . .

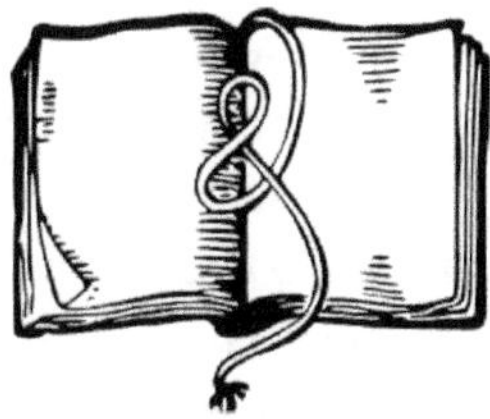

CHAPTER 9 – SECRET SOCIETIES

I include this chapter against my better judgment. Secret Societies prefer to remain so, because belonging to a plain-old society just isn't that fun.

Duck's Back Backers

Perhaps surprising to us today, Texas had long been strongly anti-alcohol. In fact, the state passed a law prohibiting the manufacture and sale of alcohol before the nation did, and it stayed on the books two years longer. A large number of Texas counties were dry from the day that Texas joined the Union, and many prohibition and temperance organizations rallied for the state-wide ban of intoxicating liquors.

A raid by masked DBB members, circa 1928.

The Duck's Back Saloon was Taylor's primary watering hole until around the time of the Great Depression, and the Duck's Back Backers worked to keep the "drys," as they called them, from shutting it down. The DBB membership largely consisted of German settlers and their descendants. Anytime anti-alcohol talk started up, they would hear about it, and take action. They donned crudely made duck-head masks, got drunk, and raided the homes and businesses of those that plotted to ban their "spirits." Soon enough, even the most sober would rarely speak their minds for fear of the duck-headed drunks. During prohibition, the Backers managed a bribe fund that kept the crazy-juice flowing behind the scenes. It was also rumored they had members in the county sheriff's department. The organization would die along with the Duck's Back Saloon in 1931.

Order of the Duck

After the change of the school's mascot from Termite to Duck, a select group of seniors chartered the Order of the Duck. Membership was granted to incoming seniors who they considered worthy. The incoming students chosen for membership took an oath to take whatever measures were necessary to protect and advance Taylor High School.

Some members have already been mentioned in this book. Albert Benson, the failed college athlete and head contractor of the New New High School, was an influential member. However, the type of students granted membership went through cycles. Most of the time the jocks held the power, but every once in a while, a powerful leader would tip the balance. When Benson took control in 1985, the Order was under jock control. However, Benson's social circle knew no bounds. He was in with the jocks, the geeks, the band nerds, the skaters, the stoners, and the goths; you could say he was Taylor's Ferris Bueller. As president, he had equal nominating power as the rest of the members combined. So, he made sure half of the class of 1986 would be non-jock. In the coming decade, the jock membership would continue to decline. Shockingly, the 2001 class was completely made up of band members.

It took another rare personality that crossed all social circles to swing the Order back to the jocks. I wasn't able to learn the identity of that particular president. Ironically, the more recent rosters are more difficult to uncover. However, by all accounts, the Order has been dominated by jocks since 2004. They have been steadfast to avoid appointing another Albert Benson by automatically disqualifying anyone in the top 10% of the class.

The Sea-Lion's Club

The Lions Club has long been active in Taylor, serving the community in many facets, not least of which was running the old putt-putt golf course in Murphy Park, which let's just say has seen better days as of this book's writing. But within the Lions Club's ranks rose a secret club within a club: the Sea-Lions. In the late 50s, the Sea-Lions started holding secret meetings in the newly formed lake on Lake Drive. They eventually contracted the Freemasons to build an underwater temple, which would eventually be covered with junk by the Collector mentioned in Chapter 5. They reinforced and expanded the temple when the island was destroyed and rebuilt. It is now only accessible by a secret entrance somewhere in Murphy Park, speculated to be on the ancient putt-putt grounds.

Each Sea-Lion member is tatooed with the Sea-Lions crest, shown here for outsiders for the first time.

What the Sea-Lions meet to discuss and plan remains secret. The Lions Club is well known for banning discussion of politics and religion, so some think this is the purpose of the Sea-Lions meetings. What impact they have had on the history of Taylor is impossible to know, but I would not be surprised if many of the occurrences in this historical account are result of their influence.

EPILOGUE

This book was written to entertain, and hopefully it has been absurd enough to do so for most readers, though I suspect only long-time Taylorians will understand some of the more obscure references.

Also, I must make clear again that this mostly fictional history is not written in offense to those that truly founded, built, and influenced Taylor history and culture. I love my hometown, and if you want to know more about it, I encourage you to research its fully true history.

As stated in the preface, a few truths are peppered amongst the make-believe. To clarify, the following pages list what was real.

Chapter 1: The Founding

- Taylor was founded in 1876.
- Taylor is between Rockdale and Round Rock.
- The facts to set the scene are all true.
- Taylor was originally named Taylorsville after a railroad official with the last name Taylor.

Chapter 2: Cotton

- Taylor was the one of the largest inland cotton markets in the early 1900s.
- The info about the first successful mechanical cotton picker is true.

- PSA: Please do not feed bread to ducks.

Chapter 3: Ducks

- Information about the "Crash at Crush" is accurate.
- Taylor originally did not have a mascot, because most schools didn't.
- Hutto's mascot is the hippo, because one did escape from a train near the town.

Chapter 4: Taylor Schools

- Info about racial segregation and integration is all true.
- Names of schools are all real.
- Taylor became the ducks due to a rainy season, and the coach's name was Drake.
- Bobby Leshikar and I were on the first Academic Decathlon team, which missed placing at state finals by seven points. The team has since won numerous state championships.
- Bobby was a teacher at Taylor High School until 2017.
- There was a band director named Rubio and the band membership and quality increased.
- Dates of the opening of school campuses and grade levels are accurate.

Chapter 5: Lake Drive

- Lake Drive was originally called Lover's Lane.
- There is a Russian-styled mansion on the west end of Lake Drive called the Clark Mansion.
- There is an island in the middle of the lake where they have launched fireworks for Independence Day.
- There were a couple years in the 90s when almost every house on Lake Drive had the described coordinated white-light decorations.

Chapter 6: Downtown

- Howard Theatre opened in 1914.
- The Theatre has opened and closed several times throughout the decades, and was open and in operation until closing

during to the COVID-19 pandemic. As of early 2023, it has not reopened.

- City National Bank is a popular local bank.
- They have a drive-thru bank at 3rd and Vance.
- Names of actual downtown businesses are accurate.

Chapter 7: Other Local Businesses

- New Orleans Shave Ice stand exists.
- Taylor Meat Company was located downtown until their current location was built.
- They sell products in stores under the “Tip-Top” brand, with the logos as described.
- Video Station opened in the mid-90s and remains the only video rental store in the area.

Chapter 8: Forgotten Hero of Taylor

- The references in the beginning are true, referring to Governor Dan Moody, Rip Torn, Bill Pickett, and Tex Avery, being from Taylor.

Chapter 9: Secret Societies

- Texas did pass prohibition laws as described.
- The Lions Club has a rule prohibiting politics and religion discussion.

Photo/Image credits:
All photos/images were taken by me, generated using DALL-E 2, or taken from public domain sources.

www.ingramcontent.com/pod-product-compliance
Ingram Content Group UK Ltd.
Pitfield, Milton Keynes, MK11 3LW, UK
UKHW020137250726
13967UKWH00002B/717

9 781008 947443